I Hate to Read!

Dedicated to our publisher, Tom Peterson,

who hates to read.

Designed by Rita Marshall

Text copyright © 1992 by Rita Marshall

Illustrations copyright © 1992 Etienne Delessert

Published in 1993 by

Creative Editions, 123 South Broad Street,

Mankato, Minnesota 56001 USA

Library of Congress Cataloging-in-Publication Data

Marshall, Rita. I hate to read/written by Rita Marshall;

illustrated by Etienne Delessert.

Summary: As a third-grader who hates to read

unwillingly looks at a book, the characters

come alive and interest him so much that

he really begins to care about them, and

begins turning the pages . . . ISBN 1-56846-005-8

[1. Books and reading—Fiction.]   I. Delessert, Etienne, ill.

II. Title.   PZ7.M356738Iah   1992   [E]—dc20   92-2693

Printed in the United States of America

Illustrations by Etienne Delessert
Story by Rita Marshall

I Hate to Read!

Creative Editions

Most of the time Victor Dickens was a really good kid.

He almost always wore his crash helmet when he practiced wheelies on his skateboard.

And once a year he allowed his mother to comb his hair with a dab of mousse for the class pictures.

He ate artichokes and liver regularly, that is to say, whenever his dog, Page, was not around at dinnertime.

· ·

Yes, most of the time Victor Dickens was a
really good kid. But Victor was a victim of the
"I Hate to Read" syndrome. He claimed it all
started when he watched Page, as a puppy, chew
up books and bury the scraps in flowerpots.

Victor got A's in math and B's in science, but F's when it came to the ABC's. Not that his family didn't try to help. His mother fed him alphabet soup for lunch. His father invested in 56 volumes of the Encyclopaedia Britannica. And his cousin Arthur read him the back of the cornflakes box every Saturday morning. But word for word, letter for letter, noodle for noodle, Victor remained a victim.

· ·

One evening while Victor was alone at his desk, pretending to read so he could watch TV, a crocodile in a white coat crawled out of the pages. "Jump into my pocket, if you like to read," he invited. "We have a story hour at 8:00."

"But I hate to read!" Victor protested. "And besides, my favorite TV show starts at 8:00."

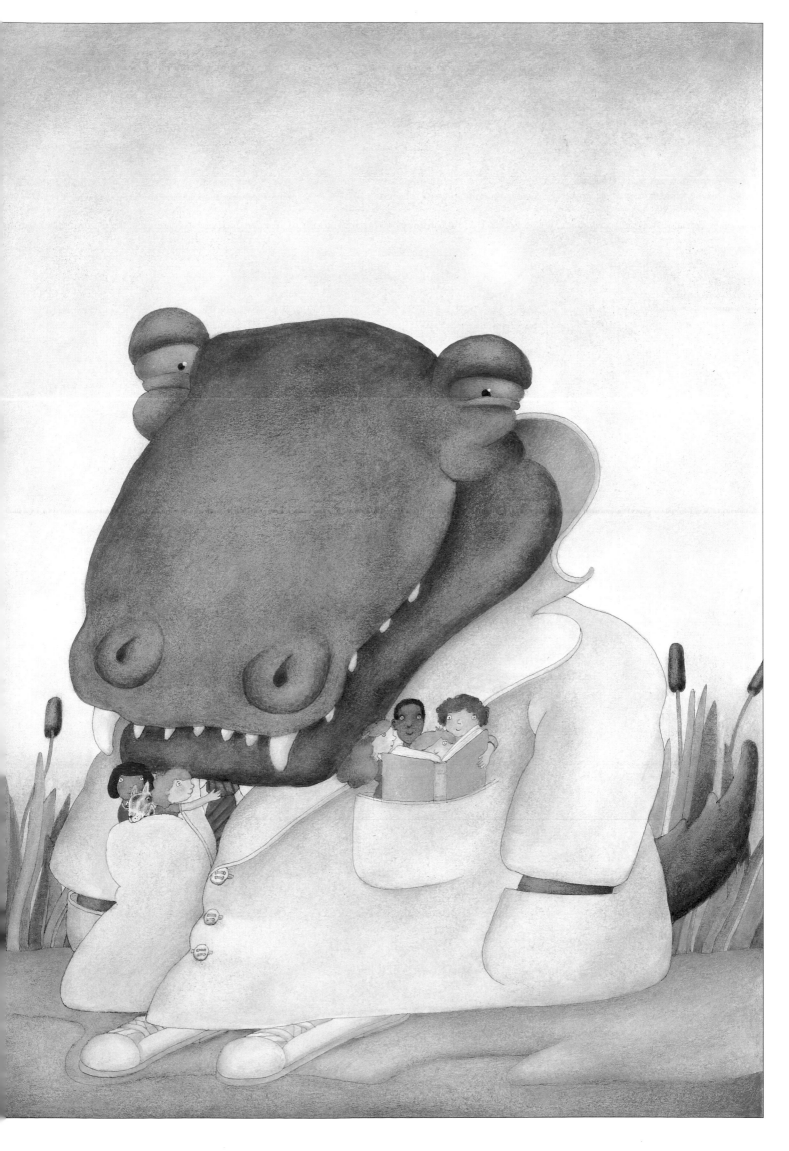

They were interrupted by a frantic little field mouse chewing her way out of the book. "Gold! Gold!" she cried at the top of her mouse lungs. "You'll find gold in this book! Plant the coins —you'll get rich! Rich with ideas and dreams!"

· ·

"My only dream is that you'll find my dad's
mousetrap on your way up to the attic!"
snapped Victor proudly.

· ·

When a weathered parrot with a pipe and a peg
leg hobbled onto the scene, Victor wondered if
he was *still* Victor W. Dickens, if he was *really*
in the third grade at Salisbury Central School,
and if Mrs. Peterson was *really* his teacher.

The parrot flipped open a rusty box with his
wooden leg. "Fly with me to the Spice Islands.
Here's a map to the hidden treasure!"

"No-o-o-o way!" said Victor, crossing his
arms in a huff. "I hate to read!"

. . . .

But before the pirate parrot could tip his hat to
say "Ahoy," a white rabbit in black barn boots
jumped out of it. "Best way to travel," he said
to Victor with a wink.

. . . .

"Come along, boy, we'll cross the Atlantic . . .
it'll be a story for *The New York Times!*"

"But I hate stories," answered Victor. "And I
hate to . . ."

. . . .

The rabbit didn't wait for him to finish. He took
a thundering leap over the house and echoed
back over his left shoulder, "Boy, you've missed
the boo-o-oot. . . ."

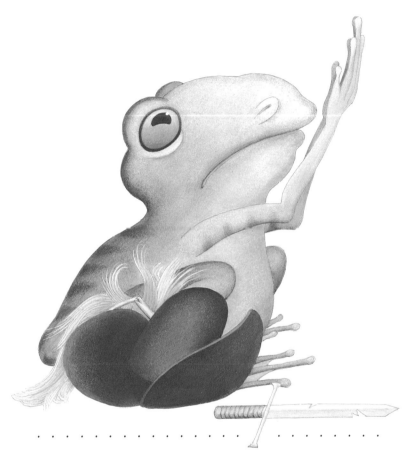

Very cautiously, Victor turned another page of the book. Out popped a slippery frog with a broken feather in his cap. "Read the page, read the page," he croaked. "Please read the page so I can turn into a prince. Then I'll kiss the Sleeping Beauty and wake her up. She's been asleep for a hundred years, you know."

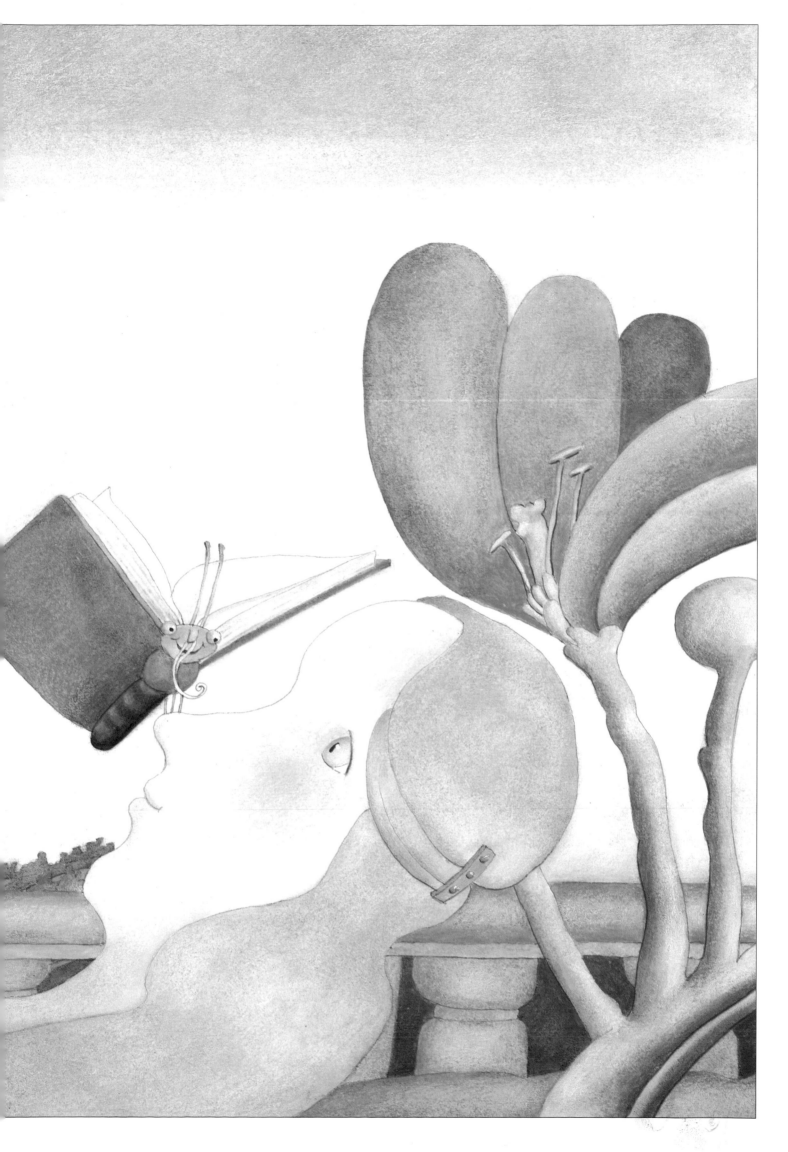

Victor turned the page. The Beauty looked just like Natalie Nickerson. And Natalie Nickerson had just invited him to her birthday party. How embarrassing! He slammed the book shut and swore never to open it again.

. . . .

It was almost dark when a strange bird appeared, tapping at the window with a glowworm in her beak. "It's fun to read, Victor Dickens," she whispered, "*even* when you're not supposed to." Now Victor loved to do things he wasn't supposed to do, but reading had never been one of them. He preferred to catch glowworms and step on them.

. . . .

By now Victor was missing his TV program, but
it didn't seem so important anymore. He closed
his eyes for a moment—and had a vision of Page
ferociously devouring books.

Then he saw Mrs. Peterson with a long nose and
a tall black hat, throwing stories into a boiling
cauldron of snakes. "We hate to read! We hate
to read!" his classmates were shouting and
stomping in unison, with Natalie Nickerson in
the lead.

. . . .

But instead of joining in the familiar chant, Victor opened his eyes and stared at the book on his desk. He thought about all the characters he'd just met and he felt a little sad—sad for the pirate and the prince, and the field mouse with the golden coins. Sad for the crocodile, and the bird in the dark, and the rabbit in the big black boots. What would happen to them if their stories were lost?

"We hate to read! We hate to read!" the chant continued. But Victor, with a smile, opened his book to look for his friends. And as he read each page, he just hated . . .

to come to the end.